FRANCES DEAN

Who Loved to Dance and Dance

TO ALL THOSE WHO LIVE
WITH ALL THEIR HEART

First published 2014 by Walker Books Ltd
87 Vauxhall Walk, London SE11 5HJ

This edition published 2015

2 4 6 8 10 9 7 5 3 1

This book has been typeset in Aunt Mildred

Printed in China

British Library Cataloguing in Publication Data:
a catalogue record for this book is available from the British Library

ISBN 978-1-4063-6079-0

www.walker.co.uk

Every one of us has the right to experience justice, fairness, freedom and truth in our lives. These important values are our human rights. Amnesty International protects people whose human rights have been taken away, and helps us all to understand our human rights better. Amnesty International has over three million members worldwide. If you would like to find out more about us and human rights education, go to **www.amnesty.org.uk** or **www.amnesty.org.au**

Who Loved to Dance and Dance

BIRGITTA SIF

WALKER BOOKS
AND SUBSIDIARIES
LONDON • BOSTON • SYDNEY • AUCKLAND

Once there was a girl,
whose name was Frances Dean.
She loved to dance and dance.

At school sometimes, while no one watched,
she danced with her fingers on her desk.
Or gently she tapped her toes to the beat
of her teacher's voice.

But mostly she couldn't wait to go
outside and dance!

When no one was around,
she would feel the wind
and dance ...

and hear the singing of the birds
and dance and dance and dance.

But when people came about,
all she could feel were their
eyes on her ...

and she forgot how to dance.

Then one day
the birds

who always loved
her dancing

showed her something
unusual.

A girl, much younger than her,
was singing the most beautiful song.

Frances Dean found herself
humming along.

That night Frances Dean couldn't sleep. She couldn't stop thinking about the little girl and how she had shared her beautiful song.

Frances Dean wondered if she would ever be able to share her dance moves like that.

The next morning when she woke,
Frances Dean felt the wind and heard
the singing of the birds.

And she was reminded with all her heart
how much she loved to dance and dance.

So while no one was around
she practised her dance moves.

And when she was ready
she let the wind move her.

And shyly she asked the birds,

"Can I show you my dance?"

She asked her cat,
"Do you know
how to dance
like this?"

She even did
a jig with the
neighbour's dog.

And when she met the old lady in the square,
she showed her how to twist.

Later on, the little girl,
with the beautiful song,
asked Frances Dean,
"Can you show me how
to dance, too?"

And she did.

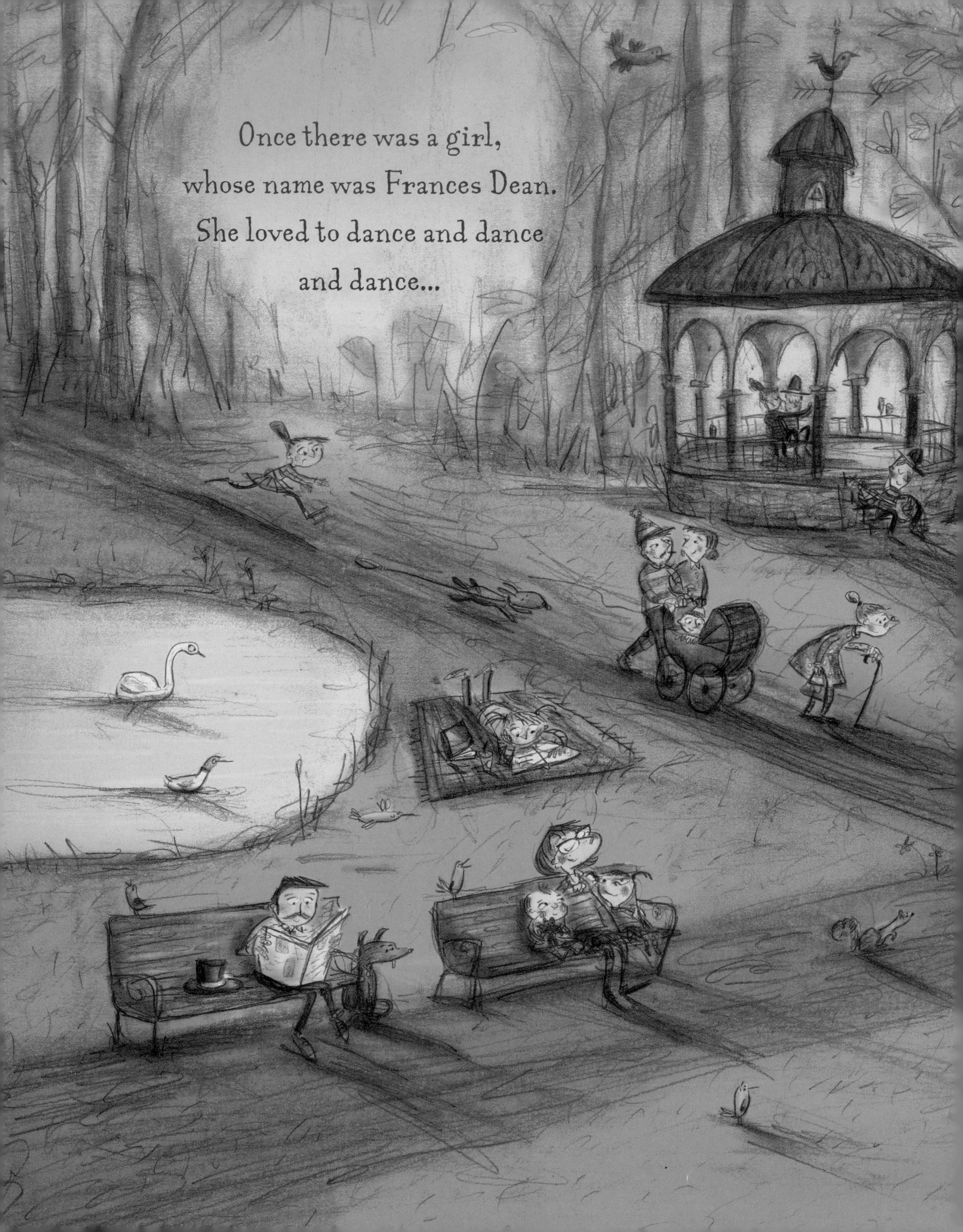
Once there was a girl,
whose name was Frances Dean.
She loved to dance and dance
and dance...